THE BIG TRIP
Up Yonder

THE BIG TRIP
Up Yonder
KURT VONNEGUT, JR.

ÆGYPAN PRESS

From *Galaxy Science Fiction,* January 1954.

Special thanks to Greg Weeks, Stephen Blundell, and the On-line Distributed Proofreading Team (which can be found at http://www.pgdp.net).

THE BIG TRIP UP YONDER
A PUBLICATION OF
ÆGYPAN PRESS

www.aegypan.com

*If it was good enough for your grandfather,
forget it . . . it is much too good for anyone else!*

Gramps Ford, his chin resting on his hands, his hands on the crook of his cane, was staring irascibly at the five-foot television screen that dominated the room. On the screen, a news commentator was summarizing the day's happenings. Every thirty seconds or so, Gramps would jab the floor with his cane-tip and shout, "Hell, we did that a hundred years ago!"

Emerald and Lou, coming in from the balcony, where they had been seeking that 2185 A.D. rarity — privacy — were obliged to take seats in the back row, behind Lou's father and mother, brother and sister-in-law, son and daughter-in-law, grandson and wife, granddaughter and husband, great-grandson and wife, nephew and wife, grandnephew and wife, great-grand-niece and husband, great-grandnephew and wife — and, of course, Gramps, who was in front of everybody. All save Gramps, who was somewhat withered and bent, seemed, by pre-anti-gerasone standards, to be about the same age — somewhere in their late twenties or early thirties. Gramps looked older because he had already reached 70 when anti-gerasone was invented. He had not aged in the 102 years since.

"Meanwhile," the commentator was saying, "Council Bluffs, Iowa, was still threatened by stark tragedy. But 200 weary rescue workers have refused to give up hope, and continue to dig in an effort to save Elbert Haggedorn, 183, who has been wedged for two days in a . . ."

"I wish he'd get something more cheerful," Emerald whispered to Lou.

"Silence!" cried Gramps. "Next one shoots off his big bazoo while the TV's on is gonna find hisself cut off without a dollar —" his voice suddenly softened and sweetened — "when they wave that checkered flag at the Indianapolis Speedway, and old Gramps gets ready for the Big Trip Up Yonder."

He sniffed sentimentally, while his heirs concentrated desperately on not making the slightest sound. For them, the poignancy of the prospective Big Trip had been dulled somewhat, through having been mentioned by Gramps about once a day for fifty years.

"Dr. Brainard Keyes Bullard," continued the commentator, "President of Wyandotte College, said in an address tonight that most of the world's ills can be traced to the fact that Man's knowledge of himself has not kept pace with his knowledge of the physical world."

"*Hell!*" snorted Gramps. "We said *that* a hundred years ago!"

"In Chicago tonight," the commentator went on, "a special celebration is taking place in the Chicago Lying-in Hospital. The guest of honor is Lowell W. Hitz, age zero. Hitz, born this morning, is the twenty-five-millionth child to be born in the hospital." The commentator faded, and was replaced on the screen by young Hitz, who squalled furiously.

"Hell!" whispered Lou to Emerald. "We said that a hundred years ago."

"I heard that!" shouted Gramps. He snapped off the television set and his petrified descendants stared silently at the screen. "You, there, boy —"

"I didn't mean anything by it, sir," said Lou, aged 103.

"Get me my will. You know where it is. You kids *all* know where it is. Fetch, boy!" Gramps snapped his gnarled fingers sharply.

Lou nodded dully and found himself going down the hall, picking his way over bedding to Gramps' room, the only private room in the Ford apartment. The other rooms were the bathroom, the living room and the wide windowless hallway, which was originally intended to serve as a dining area, and which had a kitchenette in one end. Six mattresses and four sleeping bags were dispersed in the hallway and living room, and the daybed, in the living room, accommodated the eleventh couple, the favorites of the moment.

On Gramps' bureau was his will, smeared, dog-eared, perforated and blotched with hundreds of additions, deletions, accusations, conditions, warnings, advice and homely philosophy. The document was, Lou reflected, a fifty-year diary, all jammed onto two sheets — a garbled, illegible log of day after day of strife. This day, Lou would be disinherited for the eleventh time, and it would take him perhaps six months of impeccable behavior to regain the promise of a share in the estate. To say nothing of the daybed in the living room for Em and himself.

"Boy!" called Gramps.

"Coming, sir." Lou hurried back into the living room and handed Gramps the will.

"Pen!" said Gramps.

He was instantly offered eleven pens, one from each couple.

"Not *that* leaky thing," he said, brushing Lou's pen aside. "Ah, *there's* a nice one. Good boy, Willy." He accepted Willy's pen. That was the tip they had all been waiting for. Willy, then — Lou's father — was the new favorite.

Willy, who looked almost as young as Lou, though he was 142, did a poor job of concealing his pleasure. He glanced shyly at the daybed, which would become his, and from which Lou and Emerald would have to move back into the hall, back to the worst spot of all by the bathroom door.

Gramps missed none of the high drama he had authored and he gave his own familiar role everything he had. Frowning and running his finger along each line, as though he were seeing the will for the first time, he read aloud in a deep portentous monotone, like a bass note on a cathedral organ.

"I, Harold D. Ford, residing in Building 257 of Alden Village, New York City, Connecticut, do hereby make, publish and declare this to be my last Will and Testament, revoking any and all former wills and codicils by me at any time heretofore made." He blew his nose importantly and went on, not missing a word, and repeating many for emphasis — repeating in particular his ever-more-elaborate specifications for a funeral.

At the end of these specifications, Gramps was so choked with emotion that Lou thought he might have forgotten why he'd brought out the will in the first place. But Gramps heroically brought his powerful emotions under control and, after erasing for a full minute, began to write and speak at the same time. Lou could have spoken his lines for him, he had heard them so often.

"I have had many heartbreaks ere leaving this vale of tears for a better land," Gramps said and wrote. "But the deepest hurt of all has been dealt me by —" He looked around the group, trying to remember who the malefactor was.

Everyone looked helpfully at Lou, who held up his hand resignedly.

Gramps nodded, remembering, and completed the sentence — "my great-grandson, Louis J. Ford."

"Grandson, sir," said Lou.

"Don't quibble. You're in deep enough now, young man," said Gramps, but he made the change. And, from there, he went without a misstep through the phrasing of the disinheritance, causes for which were disrespectfulness and quibbling.

*I*n the paragraph following, the paragraph that had belonged to everyone in the room at one time or another, Lou's name was scratched out and Willy's substituted as heir to the apartment and, the biggest plum of all, the double bed in the private bedroom.

"So!" said Gramps, beaming. He erased the date at the foot of the will and substituted a new one, including the time of day. "Well — time to watch the McGarvey Family." The McGarvey Family was a television serial that Gramps had been following since he was 60, or for a total of 112 years. "I can't wait to see what's going to happen next," he said.

Lou detached himself from the group and lay down on his bed of pain by the bathroom door. Wishing Em would join him, he wondered where she was.

He dozed for a few moments, until he was disturbed by someone stepping over him to get into the bathroom. A moment later, he heard a faint gurgling sound, as though something were being poured down the washbasin drain. Suddenly, it entered his mind that Em had cracked up, that she was in there doing something drastic about Gramps.

"Em?" he whispered through the panel. There was no reply, and Lou pressed against the door. The worn lock, whose bolt barely engaged its socket, held for a second, then let the door swing inward.

"Morty!" gasped Lou.

Lou's great-grandnephew, Mortimer, who had just married and brought his wife home to the Ford menage, looked at Lou with consternation and surprise. Morty kicked the door shut, but not before Lou had glimpsed what was in his hand — Gramps' enormous economy-size bottle of anti-gerasone, which had apparently been half-emptied, and which Morty was refilling with tap water.

A moment later, Morty came out, glared defiantly at Lou and brushed past him wordlessly to rejoin his pretty bride.

Shocked, Lou didn't know what to do. He couldn't let Gramps take the mousetrapped anti-gerasone — but, if he warned Gramps about it, Gramps would certainly make life in the apartment, which was merely insufferable now, harrowing.

Lou glanced into the living room and saw that the Fords, Emerald among them, were momentarily at rest, relishing the botches that the McGarveys had made of *their* lives. Stealthily, he went into the bathroom, locked the door as well as he could and began to pour the contents of Gramps' bottle down the drain. He was going to refill it with full-strength anti-gerasone from the 22 smaller bottles on the shelf.

The bottle contained a half-gallon, and its neck was small, so it seemed to Lou that the emptying would take forever. And the almost imperceptible smell of anti-gerasone, like Worcestershire sauce, now seemed to Lou, in his nervousness, to be pouring out into the rest of the apartment, through the keyhole and under the door.

*T*he bottle gurgled monotonously. Suddenly, up came the sound of music from the living room and there were murmurs and the scraping of chair-legs on the floor. "Thus ends," said the television announcer, "the 29,121st chapter in the life of your neighbors and mine, the McGarveys." Footsteps were coming down the hall. There was a knock on the bathroom door.

"Just a sec," Lou cheerily called out. Desperately, he shook the big bottle, trying to speed up the flow. His palms slipped on the wet glass, and the heavy bottle smashed on the tile floor.

The door was pushed open, and Gramps, dumbfounded, stared at the incriminating mess.

Lou felt a hideous prickling sensation on his scalp and the back of his neck. He grinned engagingly through his nausea and, for want of anything remotely resembling a thought, waited for Gramps to speak.

"Well, boy," said Gramps at last, "looks like you've got a little tidying up to do."

And that was all he said. He turned around, elbowed his way through the crowd and locked himself in his bedroom.

The Fords contemplated Lou in incredulous silence a moment longer, and then hurried back to the living room, as though some of his horrible guilt would taint them, too, if they looked too long. Morty stayed behind long enough to give Lou a quizzical, annoyed glance. Then he also went into the living room, leaving only Emerald standing in the doorway.

Tears streamed over her cheeks. "Oh, you poor lamb — *please* don't look so awful! It was my fault. I put you up to this with my nagging about Gramps."

"No," said Lou, finding his voice, "really you didn't. Honest, Em, I was just —"

"You don't have to explain anything to me, hon. I'm on your side, no matter what." She kissed him on one cheek and whispered in his ear, "It wouldn't have been murder, hon. It wouldn't have killed him. It wasn't such a terrible thing to do. It just would have fixed him up so he'd be able to go anytime God decided He wanted him."

"What's going to happen next, Em?" said Lou hollowly. "What's he going to do?"

*L*ou and Emerald stayed fearfully awake almost all night, waiting to see what Gramps was going to do. But not a sound came from the sacred bedroom. Two hours before dawn, they finally dropped off to sleep.

At six o'clock, they arose again, for it was time for their generation to eat breakfast in the kitchenette. No one spoke to them. They had twenty minutes in which to eat, but their reflexes were so dulled by the bad night that they had hardly swallowed two mouthfuls of egg-type processed seaweed before it was time to surrender their places to their son's generation.

Then, as was the custom for whoever had been most recently disinherited, they began preparing Gramps' breakfast, which would presently be served to him in bed, on a tray. They tried to be cheerful about it. The toughest part of the job was having to handle the honest-to-God eggs and bacon and oleomargarine, on which Gramps spent so much of the income from his fortune.

"Well," said Emerald, "I'm not going to get all panicky until I'm sure there's something to be panicky about."

"Maybe he doesn't know what it was I busted," Lou said hopefully.

"Probably thinks it was your watch crystal," offered Eddie, their son, who was toying apathetically with his buckwheat-type processed sawdust cakes.

"Don't get sarcastic with your father," said Em, "and don't talk with your mouth full, either."

"I'd like to see anybody take a mouthful of this stuff and *not* say something," complained Eddie, who was 73. He glanced at the clock. "It's time to take Gramps his breakfast, you know."

"Yeah, it is, isn't it?" said Lou weakly. He shrugged. "Let's have the tray, Em."

"We'll both go."

Walking slowly, smiling bravely, they found a large semi-circle of long-faced Fords standing around the bedroom door.

Em knocked. "Gramps," she called brightly, *"break*-fast is *rea*-dy."

There was no reply and she knocked again, harder.

The door swung open before her fist. In the middle of the room, the soft, deep, wide, canopied bed, the symbol of the sweet by-and-by to every Ford, was empty.

A sense of death, as unfamiliar to the Fords as Zoroastrianism or the causes of the Sepoy Mutiny, stilled every voice, slowed every heart. Awed, the heirs began to search gingerly, under the furniture and behind the drapes, for all that was mortal of Gramps, father of the clan.

*B*ut Gramps had left not his Earthly husk but a note, which Lou finally found on the dresser, under a paperweight which was a treasured souvenir from the World's Fair of 2000. Unsteadily, Lou read it aloud:

"'Somebody who I have sheltered and protected and taught the best I know how all these years last night turned on me like a mad dog and diluted my anti-gerasone, or tried to. I am no longer a young man. I can no longer bear the crushing burden of life as I once could. So, after last night's bitter experience, I say good-bye. The cares of this world will soon drop away like a cloak of thorns and I shall know peace. By the time you find this, I will be gone.'"

"Gosh," said Willy brokenly, "he didn't even get to see how the 5000-mile Speedway Race was going to come out."

"Or the Solar Series," Eddie said, with large mournful eyes.

"Or whether Mrs. McGarvey got her eyesight back," added Morty.

"There's more," said Lou, and he began reading aloud again: "'I, Harold D. Ford, etc., do hereby make, publish and declare this to be my last Will and Testament, revoking any and all former wills and codicils by me at any time heretofore made.'"

"No!" cried Willy. "Not another one!"

"'I do stipulate,'" read Lou, "'that all of my property, of whatsoever kind and nature, not be divided, but do devise and bequeath it to be held in common by my issue, without regard for generation, equally, share and share alike.'"

"Issue?" said Emerald.

Lou included the multitude in a sweep of his hand. "It means we all own the whole damn shootin' match."

Each eye turned instantly to the bed.

"Share and share alike?" asked Morty.

"Actually," said Willy, who was the oldest one present, "it's just like the old system, where the oldest people head up things with their headquarters in here and —"

"I like *that!*" exclaimed Em. "Lou owns as much of it as you do, and I say it ought to be for the oldest one who's still working. You can snooze around here all day, waiting for your pension check, while poor Lou stumbles in here after work, all tuckered out, and —"

"How about letting somebody who's never had *any* privacy get a little crack at it?" Eddie demanded hotly. "Hell, you old people had plenty of privacy back when you were kids. I was born and raised in the middle of that goddamn barracks in the hall! How about —"

"Yeah?" challenged Morty. "Sure, you've all had it pretty tough, and my heart bleeds for you. But try honeymooning in the hall for a real kick."

"*Silence!*" shouted Willy imperiously. "The next person who opens his mouth spends the next sixth months by the bathroom. Now clear out of my room. I want to think."

A vase shattered against the wall, inches above his head.

*I*n the next moment, a free-for-all was under way, with each couple battling to eject every other couple from the room. Fighting coalitions formed and dissolved with the lightning changes of the tactical situation. Em and Lou were thrown into the hall, where they organized others in the same situation, and stormed back into the room.

After two hours of struggle, with nothing like a decision in sight, the cops broke in, followed by television cameramen from mobile units.

For the next half-hour, patrol wagons and ambulances hauled away Fords, and then the apartment was still and spacious.

An hour later, films of the last stages of the riot were being televised to 500,000,000 delighted viewers on the Eastern Seaboard.

In the stillness of the three-room Ford apartment on the 76th floor of Building 257, the television set had been left on. Once more the air was filled with the cries and grunts and crashes of the fray, coming harmlessly now from the loudspeaker.

The battle also appeared on the screen of the television set in the police station, where the Fords and their captors watched with professional interest.

Em and Lou, in adjacent four-by-eight cells, were stretched out peacefully on their cots.

"Em," called Lou through the partition, "you got a washbasin all your own, too?"

"Sure. Washbasin, bed, light — the works. And we thought *Gramps'* room was something. How long has this been going on?" She held out her hand. "For the first time in forty years, hon, I haven't got the shakes — look at me!"

"Cross your fingers," said Lou. "The lawyer's going to try to get us a year."

"Gee!" Em said dreamily. "I wonder what kind of wires you'd have to pull to get put away in solitary?"

"All right, pipe down," said the turnkey, "or I'll toss the whole kit and caboodle of you right out. And first one who lets on to anybody outside how good jail is ain't never getting back in!"

The prisoners instantly fell silent.

*T*he living room of the apartment darkened for a moment as the riot scenes faded on the television screen, and then the face of the announcer appeared, like the Sun coming from behind a cloud. "And now, friends," he said, "I have a special message from the makers of anti-gerasone, a message for all you folks over 150. Are you hampered socially by wrinkles, by stiffness of joints and discoloration or loss of hair, all because these things came upon you before anti-gerasone was developed? Well, if you are, you need no longer suffer, need no longer feel different and out of things.

"After years of research, medical science has now developed *Super*-anti-gerasone! In weeks — yes, weeks — you can look, feel and act as young as your great-great-grandchildren! Wouldn't you pay $5,000 to be indistinguishable from everybody else? Well, you don't have to. Safe, tested *Super*-anti-gerasone costs you only a few dollars a day.

"Write now for your free trial carton. Just put your name and address on a dollar postcard, and mail it to 'Super,' Box 500,000, Schenectady, N. Y. Have you got that? I'll repeat it. 'Super,' Box 500,000 . . ."

Underlining the announcer's words was the scratching of Gramps' pen, the one Willy had given him the night before. He had come in, a few minutes earlier, from the Idle Hour Tavern, which commanded a view of Building 257 from across the square of asphalt known as the Alden Village Green. He had called a cleaning woman to come straighten the place up, then had hired the best lawyer in town to get his descendants a conviction, a genius who had never gotten a client less than a year and a day. Gramps had then moved the daybed before the television screen, so that he could watch from a reclining position. It was something he'd dreamed of doing for years.

"Schen-*ec*-ta-dy," murmured Gramps. "Got it!" His face had changed remarkably. His facial muscles seemed to have relaxed, revealing kindness and equanimity under what had been taut lines of bad temper. It was almost as though his trial package of *Super*-anti-gerasone had already arrived. When something amused him on television, he smiled easily, rather than barely managing to lengthen the thin line of his mouth a millimeter.

Life was good. He could hardly wait to see what was going to happen next.

— KURT VONNEGUT, JR.

www.ingramcontent.com/pod-product-compliance
Lightning Source LLC
Chambersburg PA
CBHW031906170626
46807CB00004B/1923